A Note to Parents and Caregivers:

Read-it! Readers are for children who are just starting on the amazing road to reading. These beautiful books support both the acquisition of reading skills and the love of books.

The RED LEVEL presents familiar topics using common words and repeating sentence patterns.

The BLUE LEVEL presents new ideas using a larger vocabulary and varied sentence structure.

The YELLOW LEVEL presents more challenging ideas, a broad vocabulary, and wide variety in sentence structure.

The GREEN LEVEL presents more complex ideas, an extended vocabulary range, and expanded language structures.

When sharing a book with your child, read in short stretches, pausing often to talk about the pictures. Have your child turn the pages and point to the pictures and familiar words. And be sure to reread favorite stories or parts of stories.

There is no right or wrong way to share books with children. Find time to read with your child, and pass on the legacy of literacy.

Adria F. Klein, Ph.D.
Professor Emeritus
California State University
San Bernardino, California

Managing Editor: Bob Temple
Creative Director: Terri Foley
Editor: Brenda Haugen
Editorial Adviser: Andrea Cascardi
Copy Editor: Laurie Kahn
Designer: Melissa Voda
Page production: The Design Lab
The illustrations in this book were prepared digitally.

Picture Window Books
5115 Excelsior Boulevard
Suite 232
Minneapolis, MN 55416
1-877-845-8392
www.picturewindowbooks.com

Printed in the United States of America.

Library of Congress Cataloging-in-Publication Data
Blair, Eric.
Belling the cat : a retelling of Aesop's fable / by Eric Blair ; illustrated by Dianne
Silverman.
p. cm. — (Read-it! readers)
Summary: The mice learn that "some things are easier said than done" when they try to get
rid of their great enemy the cat.
ISBN 1-4048-0321-1 (Reinforced Library Binding)
[1. Fables. 2. Folklore.] I. Aesop. II. Silverman, Dianne, ill. III. Title. IV. Series.
PZ8.2.B595 Be 2004
398.24'529353—dc22

2003016671

PICTURE WINDOW BOOKS

Belling the Cat

A Retelling of Aesop's Fable

By Eric Blair
Illustrated by Dianne Silverman

Content Adviser:
Kathy Baxter, M.A.
Former Coordinator of Children's Services
Anoka County (Minnesota) Library

Reading Advisers:
Adria F. Klein, Ph.D.
Professor Emeritus, California State University
San Bernardino, California

Susan Kesselring, M.A.
Literacy Educator
Rosemount-Apple Valley-Eagan (Minnesota) School District

Picture Window Books
Minneapolis, Minnesota

What Is a Fable?

A fable is a story that teaches a lesson. In some fables, animals may talk and act the way people do. A Greek slave named Aesop created some of the world's favorite fables. Aesop's fables have been enjoyed by readers for more than 2,000 years.

For many years, the mice had lived
in constant fear of their enemy, the cat.

Finally the mice called a meeting
to discuss how to get rid of her.

"Life would be perfect if we could
get rid of that cat," one mouse said.

The rest of the mice agreed.

9

"Can't we reason with her?"
asked a smart mouse.

"Why won't she be nice?" asked another.

One clever mouse said they should make a cat trap.

Another suggested getting a dog
to chase her away.

The mice talked for a long time.
They finally decided their problem
would be solved if they could just
hear the cat.

14

The cat was so quiet, she could sneak up on the mice.

At last, a young mouse stood up.

"Let's put a bell on a ribbon and hang it around the cat's neck," he said. "That way we'll hear her coming."

The mice were pleased with this solution.

They clapped for the simple idea.
They agreed to try it.

But one old mouse had been silent.

20

"I have a question," he finally said.
"Which one of you is going to hang
the bell on the cat's neck?" The mice
looked at one another.

"You see," said the wise old mouse,
"some things are easier said than done."

23

Levels for *Read-it!* Readers

Read-it! Readers help children practice early reading skills
with brightly illustrated stories.

 Red Level: Familiar topics with frequently used words and
repeating patterns.

 Blue Level: New ideas with a larger vocabulary and a variety
of language structures.

The Donkey in the Lion's Skin, by Eric Blair 1-4048-0320-3

The Goose that Laid the Golden Egg, by Mark White 1-4048-0219-3

 Yellow Level: Challenging ideas with an expanded vocabulary
and a wide variety of sentences.

The Ant and the Grasshopper, by Mark White 1-4048-0217-7

The Boy Who Cried Wolf, by Eric Blair 1-4048-0319-X

The Country Mouse and the City Mouse, by Eric Blair 1-4048-0318-1

The Crow and the Pitcher, by Eric Blair 1-4048-0322-X

The Dog and the Wolf, by Eric Blair 1-4048-0323-8

The Fox and the Grapes, by Mark White 1-4048-0218-5

The Tortoise and the Hare, by Mark White 1-4048-0215-0

The Wolf in Sheep's Clothing, by Mark White 1-4048-0220-7

 Green Level: More complex ideas with an extended vocabulary
range and expanded language structures.

Belling the Cat, by Eric Blair 1-4048-0321-1

The Lion and the Mouse, by Mark White 1-4048-0216-9